Marvin's

MONSTER

Diary 2

+ LYSSA!

A Note About ST₄

As a developmental pediatrician, I see children every day with problems such as anxiety, poor self-esteem, ADHD, and even screen addiction. If only these children had a set of tools available to help them address these issues! From the literature and my own clinical experience, the Stop, Take Time to Think (ST₄) series was born. Using this technique, children can learn to recognize the incredible strength they have within them—regardless of any special needs.

Imagine the sense of accomplishment that comes when children realize that they have the power to take charge of their own bodies and minds! Children can take a few moments before responding to stressful situations or acting impulsively. They can become attentive, aware, appropriate, and in short, mindful.

The heroes, the tools, and the scenarios in this series are all designed to build self-awareness and self-esteem. Readers can watch the characters grow and learn to be present in the moment. Consequently, the characters see improved behavior, gain more friends, and build happier families—which are the goals for the children reading this series, as well!

Of course, these tools are only intended to be a part of an overall treatment program, but empowering children and their families to take charge remains key.

Good luck!

Dr. Raun Melmed

Contents

CHAPTER 1

What's the Buzz?

A DAY OFF SCHOOL?!

That's what Mrs. Grimm said!

The entire class was buzzing like rumblebees after Mrs. Grimm's big announcement: the Science Scare Fair is coming up in a few weeks, and the two first-place winners will get a day off school!

Not a day off to play garbageball or Alien Universe, though. Mrs. Grimm says it's for an educational field trip of the winners' choice.

That might sound boring-snoring, but I think it sounds terrorific. The thing is, I like learning new things.

One time my momster took me to a museum that had a lot of ancient monster bones. I didn't think I'd like it, but I learned every name of every dragosaur! The tour guide was impressed.

And one time, my popster took me to work with him for Take Your Minor Monster to Work Day. He works at a laboratory as a fumeist—he mixes and burns and freezes things. He even let me (with proper eye protection) pour a purple liquid into a green one and watch it explode!

Really, learning isn't so bad. But sometimes during class I just get a little . . . distracted.

Sometimes I see something across the room and my mind totally runs off in another direction in a pair of Sneaky, Squeaky Sneakers.

Going somewhere like a museum or a concert or the zoo instead of to school sounds CLAWESOME! Sometimes I need to get up and DO something instead of sitting at my desk all day. And even though I'd be learning, I bet it would feel a little like a vacation too.

I've GOT to win the grand prize!

I just need the perfect project and the perfect partner.

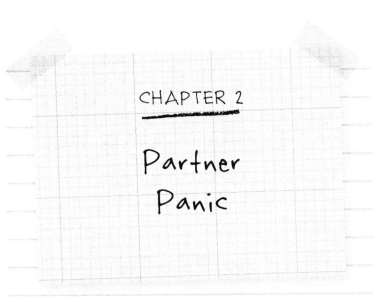

CHAPTER 2

Partner Panic

After Mrs. Grimm's announcement at the beginning of fumeistry class, it was time to partner up. I turned to my friend Timmy Tentacle to ask if he would be my partner. But he was already partners with Harriet Hairstein, who goes by Ari.

Darn! Timmy and Ari are my two closest friends. Who else was I supposed to team up with?

Everyone else quickly grabbed a buddy, and before I knew it, I was one of the last monsters left. Then I noticed the new girl, Lyssa S. Lug (yes, she introduced herself with the S!), sitting in a corner of the room, looking very busy with her fumeistry notes.

Then I remembered what happened during recess yesterday. I wondered if the class was avoiding her as much as she was avoiding them.

Here's what happened:

A whole bunch of monsters were getting ready to play an atrociously fun game called shoeball. Everyone on the field wears only one shoe. Monsters on each team try to run past each other without getting their shoe stolen. (If you do, you have to sit out for ten seconds, then go back to the middle of the field and try again.) You can also dodge other players or block them from getting by. When you get to the end of the field, you can score points—by flinging your shoe off your foot into a net!

Tyler Terror invited Lyssa to play on our team.

"No thanks," she said. She was reading a book instead. It looked like our histroary textbook.

"Don't bother," Nella Nasty told Tyler. "She'd rather stick her snout in a book all day. I bet she doesn't even know how to play!"

Lyssa glared at her. "I do TOO know how to play!"

Nella and her friends just laughed.

Lyssa slammed her book closed and marched up to Tyler. "As a matter of fact, I WILL play." And she did!

Well, sort of.

She began with both shoes off, for starters. After she remembered to put one shoe back on, the game was

You show 'em, Lyssa!

already in full force—there were monsters everywhere! Running and dodging and grabbing for shoes! Lyssa joined back in but didn't seem to know where to go or who was on her team.

At one point, Lyssa grabbed for Arika
Arachne's shoe . . .

. . . but one of Arika's eight bare feet
stepped on her hand.

Then I saw Lyssa trying to get past the
other team, so I blocked Heidi Horrible
from stealing Lyssa's shoe. Lyssa made
it past, ran to the end of the field, and
flung—but her shoe didn't come off. Felix
Furryman stole the shoe right off her foot!

"Loosen your shoelaces. It helps," I offered helpfully as she skulked by on her way to the sideline. She told me to mind my own business.

Then, when Lyssa was back in, Nella Nasty ran HARD into Lyssa and knocked her to the ground. Nella snickered.

That did it. Lyssa leapt up unsteadily,
stumbled toward the end of the field past
opponents and teammates alike, wound up,
and kicked—and her shoe went in!

She whooped and pumped her clawfist and
turned to Nella. "See? I can play as well
as you!" She stuck out her tongue.

Nella snorted a laugh. "Too bad that was YOUR team's shoeball net."

The other team guffawed. Lyssa's face fell. She looked to our team to see if it was true. It was.

Her face crumpled with tears, then something else. She began turning pink, then red, then purple—but not because she was a chameleon monster.

Lyssa exploded. Okay, she didn't
ACTUALLY explode—but she shrieked
the LOUDEST shriek I've ever heard. And
I've heard a lot of shrieks—after all, I
AM a monster!

She lobbed her shoe at no one in
particular. She kicked the hoop with a
hollow THWONG! as her socked foot
collided painfully with the pole.

Then she started pounding her clawfists on the ground, shrieking and crying. Mrs. Grimm arrived to escort her inside.

The silent playground just stared.

BACK IN FUMEISTRY CLASS

"Hey, uh, do you want to be my partner?" I asked.

Lyssa looked up in surprise. In fact, she looked stunned! "Sure," she said softly.

"Clawesome, dude!" I said, flashing a MONSTER ON! hand gesture.
That made me think about Monster Rock, so I started playing air guitar.

She raised an eyebrow. I hoped she wouldn't start turning colors again.

I wasn't sure how teaming up with Lyssa was going to go, but I knew I was up for the challenge.

I'm up for the challenge!

CHAPTER 3

Storming Our Brains

"One rule: No explosions for the sake of explosions! Any explosions should be controlled and must have a scientific purpose," Mrs. Grimm explained.

"Boring-snoring!" I called out.

Mrs. Grimm crossed all her arms across her chest and glared. Others in the class giggled.

"Sorry," I said, grinning like an imp.

Mrs. Grimm told us that every partnership needed to come up with an idea for their Scare Fair project by the end of the week and tell her about it. It was Tuesday, so that gave us four days. She even gave us time during class to brainstorm with our partners.

"How about a giant monster-putty volcano?" I suggested. I was dreaming of a foamy, frothy explosion.

"No," Lyssa said. "Everyone does those."

I wondered how she knew that . . .

"We could compare and contrast different rocks and their properties," Lyssa suggested.

Boring-snoring. Maybe she was trying to look smart. But I zipped my lips and didn't say that. "Maybe," I said instead.

We stormed our brains until the end-of-class bell screeched. We'd come up with a big nothing.

"Let's think about it for a few days," Lyssa suggested. I agreed.

I tried to think of ideas during my other classes, but I couldn't do that AND listen to Mrs. Grimm. We were learning about Priya Pixie's histroaric battle against a cyclops at the War of Wet Waters. I imagined myself fighting a giant cyclops. I thought about slingshots and catapults and flaming arrows and . . . EXPLOSIONS! But Mrs. Grimm said no unnecessary explosions. Sigh.

"Is my lesson boring you, Marvin?"

Mrs. Grimm was hovering right over me.
I hadn't noticed her there because I was
daydreaming. Everyone was watching me.

"No!" I bolted straight up. "I'm sorry, I
was just—uh . . ."

But Mrs. Grimm didn't yell. She didn't turn purple. She didn't give me a red-spike sticker. She simply pointed to something on my desk—my ST$_4$ badge.

Right. I just needed to Stop, Take Time to Think.

ST_4

Stop
Take
Time
To
Think

ST_4

That's what ST_4 means—it's my secret formula that reminds me to stop and focus on what is happening around me when my mind is going a million monster-feet a minute.

It helps me be in charge of myself. My momster calls it "being mindful." But I came up with ST_4 on my own—most people don't know about it. Only me, my parents, Mrs. Grimm, Timmy, and Ari are in on it. When I taught it to Timmy and Ari, they thought it was way cool and started to use it too!

One other trick I use is called a
"monstercam." Stevie Strummer (my
musical hero) taught it to me. I make a
rectangle with my fingers—just like this!—
and focus that rectangle on whatever I
should be paying attention to.

When I used my monstercam during histroary class, I saw "MEATY TREATY OF 1350" written on the board. I flipped open my histroary book to the correct page and focused on listening to Mrs. Grimm.

I couldn't think about my science project and histroary at the same time! I'd have to wait until I got home to think about the Scare Fair.

CHAPTER 4

Advice from a Scientist

That afternoon, I sat at my desk with my three-claw binder and a pencil. The top of my paper said SCIENCE SCARE FAIR IDEAS—and nothing else! This was going to be HARD.

I chewed on the end of my pencil. Of course! I knew the problem—I couldn't think on an empty stomach!

So I tromped down the stairs, scarfed down one (or maybe two) of Momster's delicious boo-berry muffins, and returned to my room.

My tummy was full, but my paper was not. My brain was plenty full—just not with any science project ideas!

Brain Food

So instead, I did my monsterology homework. I played my baby fang guitar. I skittered into Molly's room and flipped her picture frames upside down. I danced around my room to Monster Rock, my favorite band. I put a fake butterfly under Molly's pillow and cackled. Molly HATES butterflies. I stomped around in circles.

STILL no ideas!

"Why don't you take a prowl around the block?" Popster suggested. "Get the brain mucus flowing."

I didn't see how that could help.

"Everything is science, son. There are natural wonders all around you."

I didn't want to go on a prowl. I could think about the project tomorrow, I decided. I'd been thinking hard all day, and I just wanted to watch Super Scarers until I couldn't keep my eyes open.

So that's what I did. Of course, nothing got done.

The next afternoon was Thursday, and I HAD to come up with some ideas to share with Lyssa on Friday. I didn't want her to think I was lazy.

After I finished my other homework, I remembered my popster's words: "Everything is science, son. There are natural wonders all around you."

I didn't know what he meant, but he IS a scientist, so he must know what he's talking about. I had nothing better to do, anyway— why not go for a prowl?

What do you have to lose?

So that's what I did.

I formed a rectangle with my fingers, and I was amazed at what my monstercam came up with.

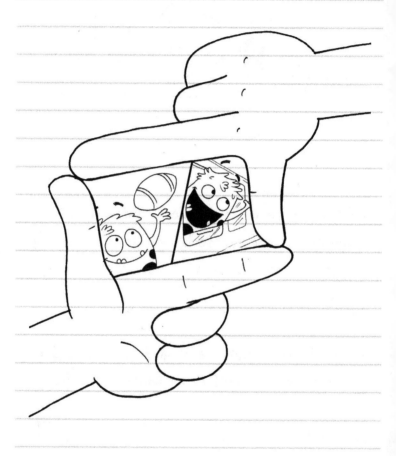

CHAPTER 5

The Neighborhood Prowl

Oh my! Right at the start of my prowl, I saw some monsters playing garbageball. That did it. Let's just say I forgot all about the Scare Fair for a while.

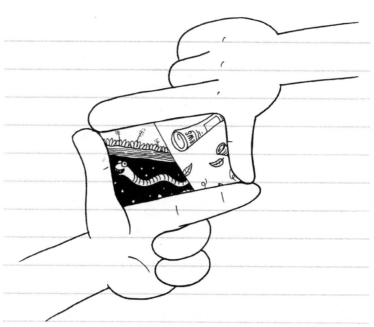

After the game, I thought about how
my popster always says he wishes he could
bottle my energy. Now THAT would be a
great science project—if only I knew how!

On the way home, I tried focusing my
monstercam on things all around me, one by
one. Suddenly, I started REALLY noticing
and wondering about things. Dirtworms—
why do they live in the dirt? What made
ring-swings, you know, swing? Why can the
wind carry a piece of papernews but not
carry me?

I still needed a first-place idea. I wanted Lyssa to see that I meant business about this project. She's smart and good at science—she always gets gold spike stickers in fumeistry class—but I wanted her to see that I am, too. I may get red spikes sometimes, and I may daydream during class, but I AM smart!

More questions popped into my mind. Why does water run downhill? What makes frightcycles rust? How does a house stand up? Why does food rot?

My brain mucus was definitely flowing now! I scurried all the way home to begin writing down my ideas.

Do brains really have mucus?

Now I had too many ideas! And I liked them all!

Would Lyssa be impressed? Or would she think I was trying to show off? I didn't want her to think I was TRYING to impress her. But I didn't want her to think I was goofing off, either. Most of all, I just didn't want to make her mad!

"What's on the paper?" Timmy asked me on the bus the next morning when he saw me pondering my list of ideas. I told him I was trying to come up with a Scare Fair project.

"I think Ari and I are going to make a monster-putty volcano," he said. I didn't tell him what Lyssa had to say about that.

I watched over his shoulder as he played Alien Universe. My mind was totally off in outer space, just like his monsternaut character. My brain was getting fuzzy from working so hard. I wished I could climb in a rocket and launch myself into outer space so I wouldn't have to think about the Scare Fair anymore!

Outer space. Hmm . . .

CHAPTER 6

A Shiny Idea

I was still thinking about that rocket launching into space when I saw Lyssa at school.

She had some monstrously good ideas. Like hatching baby featherfiend eggs or building a shocktrical circuit to charge a zaplet. She thought we could study spleenus flytraps and find out what they will and won't eat.

I was nervous to tell her my ideas. And I was still thinking about that rocket.

That's when I realized something brilliant—our project should be a real, launchable rocket!

Lyssa agreed it was brilliant.

In fact, she said, "Marvin, that's BRILLIANT!"

"You don't think everyone else will do it too?" I asked, thinking of the monster-putty volcano.

"No," she said. "Building a rocket that actually launches is difficult, so a lot of monsters won't even try it."

I didn't even think about it being hard.
Oh, great.

Lyssa saw my worried look. "Don't worry,
Marvin. Science is my best subject. I've
got tons of ideas for how we can do this.
And I've seen your fumeistry experiments
in class—when you're not spacing out,
you're pretty good at science."

I felt embarrassed . . . and proud. "Thanks,
I think."

I was glad Lyssa was my partner—
because even though I had this scaryific
idea, I had no idea how we were going to
do it!

Mrs. Grimm loved our idea and wished us
luck!

Lyssa and I got to work right away. I began sketching out what our rocket might look like. While I sketched, we stormed our brains of everything we knew about rockets. (Lyssa knew a LOT more than I did!) We scratched down things we wanted to find out for our informational poster.

"Can I see what you drew?" Lyssa asked after we finished brainstorming.

When I showed her, she frowned. "No, no, that's all wrong. It has too many corners."

"I thought it could be robot themed. We could paint it metallic gray and give it a little antenna," I said, pointing to the antenna I drew.

"The top needs to be pointy but round," she said. "And it needs fins to be more aerodynamic—not legs!" She harrumphed and drew a giant X through my drawing.

"Hey!" I protested. "You didn't have to do that!"

"You have to take this more seriously."

"I am!"

"Doesn't seem like it," she snapped.

I slumped in my chair and watched her sketch. She explained why each thing she drew would help the rocket launch better. Even though I felt like she was smashing my ideas with a pretend monster wrecking ball, I had to admit she was making sense.

While Lyssa worked, I daydreamed about winning the Scare Fair. I imagined launching our shiny rocket with a dramatic puff of smoke, the rocket shooting so high that it sailed straight into outer space. I imagined the judges and our classmates clapping and cheering, giving us medals and flowers, and lifting Lyssa and me up onto their shoulders.

"Marvin!"

I jumped. Lyssa was staring at me.
I grinned my shy smile. "Sorry. I get
distracted."

"I noticed! I said you should come over
this weekend so we can start building the
rocket."

CHAPTER 7

A Dark, Dark Cave

We worked on our rocket all week! Lyssa's momster helped us cut things with a saber-tooth saw, but Lyssa and I did all the planning, tracing, fitting, and gluing.

I learned that Lyssa doesn't just like science—she likes music too, like me! She plays the drum-bone-o-phone. One of  her favorite places to go is Monsterland, with all its speeding looper coasters and dizzy spinning-top rides. She said she was supposed to go there with her dad, but she hadn't seen him in a while.

Wow! Making the rocket with Lyssa was a lot of fun! But it wasn't ALWAYS. Some nights I got bored and just wanted to lay my head on the table and take a nap.

"Wake up, Marvin," Lyssa would say in a sing-songy voice. "Keep your eyes on the prize!" So I'd take out my monstercam and focus on the rocket.

Sometimes Lyssa would get really frustrated when two parts wouldn't fit. "It looks so stupid. I can't do anything right," she'd say. Her ears would turn red or purple or orange. She'd stare fiercely at whatever she was doing, like she was trying to use Super Scarer heat vision to melt it.

I felt bad when she said things like that because I thought our project looked amazing, especially the parts Lyssa did. "It doesn't look stupid! It looks better than anything I could do. Look!" I'd say, and I'd glue leftover pieces of foam to my eyebrows or my shirt or my arm. "Do I look like a rocket now?"

Her shoulders would relax, and her mouth would quirk up in a smile. She'd shake her head like I was being ridiculous. But it always made her smile.

Soon enough, with only a week to go until the big day, our rocket looked like a rocket! The only thing left was to decorate it and create our poster.

Lyssa asked if I wanted to decorate it because art was her worst subject. I wasn't that great at art either, but wow! It was the first time Lyssa asked me to handle something by myself. It was nice to know she trusted me. So, I agreed. I had some truly scaryific colors in mind that I hoped she'd love!

I took it home and sketched and painted all weekend. (At least, it felt like all weekend!) The rocket turned out truly spooktacular. I couldn't wait to show Lyssa.

That Monday may have been the worst
day of my life.

The Science Scare Fair wasn't here yet,
but I just couldn't wait to show Lyssa my
artistic genius. I took the rocket with me
to school so I could show her. On the bus,
I showed the rocket to Timmy, who seemed
frightfully impressed.

I wished I would have used ST_4 then,
because I took it a little far—like I
always do. As we pulled into the school
parking lot, I hung out the bus window and
flew the rocket through the air more like a
scareplane than a rocket.

But then the bus hit a speed lump in the road.

And I dropped our amazing rocket.

And the bus behind us ran over it.

I wanted to crawl into a dark, dark cave and never come out.

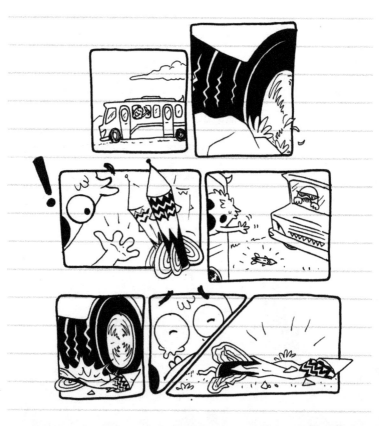

CHAPTER 8

Nuclear Meltdown

I REALLY wished I had known where the nearest cave was, because telling Lyssa was probably the scariest thing I've ever done. And not scary in a good way.

"You DESTROYED our rocket?!?!?!?!?" she shrieked.

She'd been perfectly calm only moments before, but now she was turning pink, then orange, then purple, then yellow. She slammed her fists on her desk over and over, louder and louder. Soon the whole class was looking. She knocked all her books onto the floor. Then she knocked all MY books to the floor. I told her over and over how sorry I was, but she couldn't hear me through her screaming.

"Lyssa!" Mrs. Grimm gasped. But then Lyssa was sobbing. Mrs. Grimm glared at me. "You two. See me in the hallway."

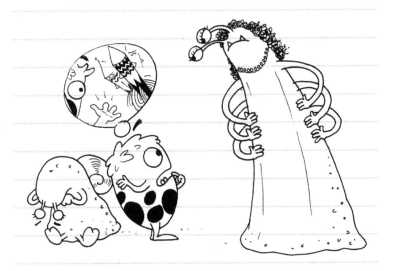

Lyssa kept crying, so I had to tell Mrs. Grimm what happened. I swore it was an accident.

"An accident, maybe, but it sounds like you were being reckless, Marvin," Mrs. Grimm said sternly. "You should have thought about what you were doing. You should have used ST_4."

I didn't know it was possible to feel any lower than I already felt.

"However," Mrs. Grimm said, "you still have a few days to redo the project. Is any of the rocket still usable?"

I held up the smashed mess.

Mrs. Grimm pursed her lips. "Perhaps not."

Lyssa sobbed louder and then exploded into more screams—just like that time on the playground.

I felt terrible about what happened, but I felt even worse that I made her feel this awful. I desperately wished there was something I could do right then.

"Well, I cannot give you more time because the Science Scare Fair is happening this Friday, no matter what. You two will have to do your best to make it again."

Lyssa croaked something: "I'm not working with him anymore."

Apparently, it WAS possible to feel lower.

CHAPTER 9

Starting Over

Lyssa wouldn't talk to or even look at me for the rest of the day. She had every right to be mad at me. I was mad at me!

Momster knew something was wrong the moment I walked through the door after school. Dropping onto one of our hairy sofas, I told her everything: my terrible mistake, Lyssa's reaction, our talk with Mrs. Grimm. I even admitted that I was a little scared of Lyssa and told her about the other times Lyssa had gotten mad at me.

"I understand why she's angry right now," I said. "I wish I had a time machine to undo it! But Timmy and Harriet have never been this mad at me, and I've known them longer!"

"Everyone handles angry feelings differently," Momster explained. "It sounds like Lyssa is dealing with a lot. She just moved here, which probably means she's adjusting to a lot of new things. Anger might be the way she expresses her frustrations and worries, like how Harriet sometimes breathes fast or cries when she's worried."

I'd have to think about that. But then my mind turned back to the Scare Fair. "But what am I supposed to do about my project?" I moaned. I imagined showing up to the event with a great big box of nothing and a poster saying MARVIN RUINED EVERYTHING!

"I can't make another rocket without her. She's the one who figured out how to actually do it." I stuffed a pillow over my face and groaned.

"Try apologizing to Lyssa again," Mom said.

"She won't talk to me."

"Give her some time to de-monsterate. To cool off."

I wasn't counting on Lyssa forgiving me that soon. I was going to have to start another project from scratch.

I spent all evening looking over my old list of ideas for a science project. They were all boring-snoring compared to our rocket. None would win me first place. But I needed a project no matter what, or I'd get an F in fumeistry.

bye bye
first place
...

I looked at my ST$_4$ badge stuck to the wall over my desk, reminding me again to stop, take time to think.

I tried to remember all the steps for making the rocket, but I couldn't remember all the details and measurements. There was no way around it: I needed Lyssa if I wanted to make a rocket.

Why couldn't Lyssa understand that what I did was an accident? If SHE'D been the one to break it, I would be sad, but I would understand. But then I remembered what Momster said about how Lyssa expressed her feelings. I guess just because I don't get as angry doesn't mean someone else won't.

Everyone expresses their feelings differently

I began reading about real space rockets on my zaplet. I didn't understand a lot of the super sciency stuff. But I did learn about how rockets launch, travel through Monstearth's atmosphere, orbit, and land. And I learned about temperature control. Rockets can't launch without heat, but if everything gets too hot, the rocket might explode!

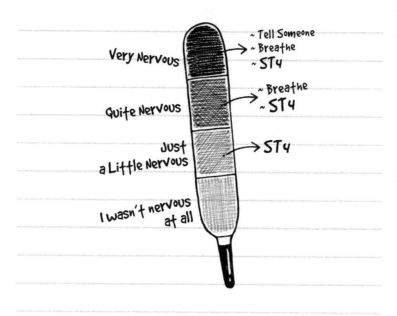

This made me think of Ari's fearometer. (It looks just like the fearometer my popster sticks under my tongue when I'm sick!) She uses it when she gets stressed or anxious. The fearometer is split into four sections—green (meaning Not Anxious), yellow, orange, and red (meaning EXTREMELY Anxious). She chooses which color represents her feelings, and each color tells her something to do to help her calm down, like counting to ten or breathing deeply.

Or telling someone about it. Or taking a prowl—or even a shower!

All of this reminded me of Lyssa. Maybe her temper gets too hot sometimes and she doesn't know how to cool it down because she doesn't have something like Ari's fearometer.

Hmm... maybe a fearometer could help!

When I went to bed that night, I felt like I understood Lyssa a little better. But I still didn't know what to do about my project.

CHAPTER 10

Nuclear
Cleanup

I was still no closer to a new project. I was beginning to get anxious. What if I never came up with one? I'd get a big fat F and maybe some red spikes from Mrs. Grimm. And NO day off school.

RED SPIKE STICKER

Lyssa	
Marvin	△△△△
Harriet	△△
Penelope	△△
Lily	△△
Timmy	△△
Kevin	△

Too Many to Count!

SCARE FAIR PROJECT

F.

During fumeistry on Tuesday, Mrs. Grimm gave us time to work on our projects. I noticed Lyssa sitting alone in the corner—I guess she hadn't gotten a new partner. Sitting there, she didn't look mad. She just looked sad.

Then I decided something. Even if Lyssa didn't want to work with me, I was still going to try to be her friend. I missed talking to her. She really could be heaps of fun, whenever she wasn't mad. And she could probably use a friend.

So I took a chance and walked right up to
her, sat down, and apologized! I told her I
was sorry that I didn't take time to think
about what I was doing when I stuck
the rocket out the window. I said that I
understood if she was mad still and didn't
want to work with me, but I still wanted
to be her friend.

"I actually wanted to apologize to you,"
she said.

Apologize to ME?

"I shouldn't have yelled at you and knocked over your books and gotten so mad at you when it was just an accident."

Then in a whisper so other monsters couldn't hear, she told me that the night before, she was so stressed and frustrated and sad that she cried and screamed and said mean things to her momster. Amazingly, her momster didn't punish her or take away her zaplet!

"I thought I could do the project by myself, but I was getting too stressed. When my momster saw how upset I was, she told me I needed my partner back. She's right. I can't do it all by myself. You're good at making me laugh and helping me not feel so worried about our project."

Then she told me that moving here was hard because she missed her old friends, old house, and old school, and she missed her dad. Her parents weren't together anymore. She said she felt lonely because she hadn't made any friends yet.

"I would be really sad too if I had to deal with all of that. But I can be your friend—if you're okay with it," I offered.

She smiled. "Of course! Can . . . can we be science partners again too?"

I thought she'd never ask!

CHAPTER 11

Explosion Control, Part 1

We got right back to work. We had a lot to do! One night Lyssa suddenly slapped her pencil on the table and dropped her head in her hands. "How in all of badness are we going to pull this off? There's too much to do in just a few days. Stupid Scare Fair!" she flung her pencil across the room. I moved out of the way just in time.

"It's okay, Lyssa. We've made one rocket already, so it should be easier the second time. We'll be able to do it faster!"

"But our first rocket was scaryific. How are we going to make another one as good?" She started to cry. "We have to get more supplies and then measure and trace and cut everything again . . . And if it's not perfect, the rocket might EXPLODE."

I loved a good explosion, but that was not an explosion I wanted! I put my claw on her shoulder. "I know we can do this! We've already researched everything. We'll know exactly what each piece should look like. Think about the first one as a practice rocket!"

She sighed. "Maybe you're right. I just get so angry and frustrated sometimes about lots of little things and big things. I don't know what to do. It's like my feelings are mashed into a monster-putty volcano, ready to explode at any time."

I imagined climbing a ginormous volcano and feeling it rumble under my feet, then the volcano shooting hot lava straight into the air.

Then it came to me. "Or . . . like a rocket?" I carefully picked up our rocket. "Your feelings get all trapped into a small space, like a rocket engine—then something lights it up and shoots it off." I lifted our rocket straight into the air like it was launching.

"Exactly," Lyssa said.

Then it occurred to me that I should tell Lyssa about ST_4.

"What's ST_4?" she asked when I mentioned it.

"It's this fumeical formula I use to help me focus on what I'm supposed to do. The S stands for STOP, and the four Ts stand for TAKE TIME TO THINK. I stop to think about what I'm supposed to be doing and imagine myself doing that instead of whatever I'm actually doing. Maybe it can help you think about why you feel angry."

Lyssa said she would try it.

We decided to take a break, so I showed her how to make ST_4 stickers. Lyssa used waxsticks to draw her sticker in the shape of a rocket. They looked terrorifically cool!

Then Lyssa looked thoughtful. "I think I felt angry just now because I'm nervous we won't be able to finish in time," Lyssa said. "I really want to win first place."

"Me too. I'm sorry I made us lose important time," I said, feeling sorry for myself.

"It's okay, Marvin." Lyssa smiled. "But maybe this time I'LL take the rocket to school—just in case."

our rocket tucked safe and snug in there

CHAPTER 12

Yikes Spikes

To both of our surprise, I turned out to be right: making the rocket WAS easier the second time. It was the day before the Science Scare Fair, and we'd had just enough time to finish our new rocket and our poster. Lyssa came up with some ghoulishly good ideas to take our poster to the next level, or "into the stratosphere," as Lyssa said. I was so excited to present our project at the Scare Fair.

The stratosphere is one of the layers of Monstearth's atmosphere

Lyssa didn't seem so excited, though. During math that morning, Lyssa kept her head down on the desk the whole time and didn't do any work. Then in histroary class, Mrs. Grimm called on Lyssa to answer a question, but Lyssa didn't say anything, even when Mrs. Grimm asked her to simply guess. Mrs. Grimm gave her a red spike for her "poor attitude." Lyssa didn't seem to care.

Something must have been wrong with Lyssa. She always pays attention in class! Did she sleep monstrously last night? Did she forget to eat breakfast?

Later, in fumeistry class, I asked her what was wrong.

"Nothing. Leave me alone."

I was stunned. Was she mad at me again? I thought about the last time I saw her: we were putting the finishing touches on our project. She didn't seem mad at me then. She seemed excited!

She sighed. I saw her stop and take time to think. "I guess I'm so nervous about the Scare Fair that I can't focus on anything else. I know our project is good, but I don't think it's quite perfect. I wish we had more time." She looked at her claws, folded on the desk. "I've never gotten a red spike before."

I assured her that they weren't so bad. You had to get three before you missed recess. "Hey, I know our project is going to ROCKET!" I grinned. "Get it? ROCK it?"

Lyssa rolled her eyes but giggled.

"My friend Ari is coming over after school. Do you want to come too?" Now that we were done with our project, I thought Lyssa could use some fun.

"I don't know . . . Maybe I should put some finishing touches on our poster."

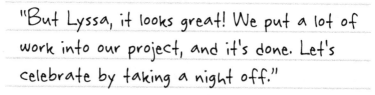

What a relief!
Time for some fun!

"But Lyssa, it looks great! We put a lot of work into our project, and it's done. Let's celebrate by taking a night off."

She agreed!

CHAPTER 13

The Party's Over—
Too Soon

That afternoon, Lyssa was first to arrive. She looked upset. I asked her what was wrong, but she said, "Nothing. It's nothing."

"Let's draw with slimewalk chalk," I suggested. We doodled all over the slimewalk, and Ari arrived a few minutes later.

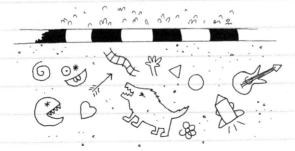

"I like your manglemane lion, Lyssa," Ari said. "They're my favorite!"

"It's a rarewolf," Lyssa corrected. "Not a lion."

Ari blushed and apologized. "It looks great!"

"No, it doesn't," Lyssa said. "Not if you thought it was a lion." She scribbled it out.

Later we played a game I call Lava Leap.
You must cross the yard by hopping onto
whatever you can to stay off the grass,
which I pretend is lava. I usually leave a
lot of my stuff in the yard, so you can
hop from rock to fizzbee to dirt patch
to picnic blanket, and it's freaky fun!
Whoever gets to the other side, wins!

We raced toward the fence on the other
side of the yard, hopping like fuzzy little
monsteroos. We were all laughing because
it was so much fun! Lyssa almost made it
to the other side until she slipped off the
skateboard she was balancing on.

"You're out, Lyssa!" I bellowed like a batball umpire. Ari made one last hop and touched the fence at the far end of the yard, whooping and cheering.

I finally made it to the other side and yelled, "SECOND PLACE!" I high-foured Ari and did a little dance. It took me a little too long to realize that Lyssa was sitting in the grass, arms folded tight across her chest, frowning.

"It's not fair!" she whined. "I fell over!"

"That's part of the challenge, Lyssa!" I explained.

"You play this all the time, so you're better at it!"

"It's okay—it's just a game. It's fun to play even if you don't win," I said.

"Not for me," she said. She got up and stomped around the corner of the house, out of sight.

"I didn't mean to hurt her feelings," Ari said, worried. "I don't care if I win. She probably hates me now. First, I called her wolf a lion. Then I beat her at Lava Leap—"

"I'm sure she doesn't hate you," I tried to comfort Ari. But she still looked worried and nervous. She sat down and hugged her knees.

Now I had two upset friends. Today was not as fun as I'd hoped.

"Maybe if I apologize to Lyssa, she won't hate me," Ari said. "Or maybe she doesn't hate me, but just had a really hard day or something." She got to her feet. "I'm going to go apologize."

"Wait," I said. "I have an idea."

I think someone just used ST4!

CHAPTER 14

Explosion Control, Part 2

In the end, Ari and I both apologized. Lyssa sighed. "I'm sorry too. I reacted too fast and was mean about it. I know it's just a game."

We told her it was okay.

"I just needed to be alone so I could cool off. I call it a 'time-in.' When I feel mad or sad, I walk away and think about a happy place so I can calm down and think," she explained. "I guess it's kind of like ST_4 in a way. I even have a time-in spot at home where I can curl up, or pound a pillow,

or squish some modeling slime. Now that I've had a time-in, I feel a lot calmer already."

"Wow, Lyssa! That's a monsterific idea!" Ari said.

I told Lyssa that Ari uses ST_4 too.

"It's true," Ari said. "Marvin told me about it. I like to think of a happy place, just like you do, and take deep breaths when I'm nervous or upset." Ari took a slow, deep breath. Her shoulders scrunched up when she inhaled and relaxed when she exhaled.

Lyssa tried it. "Wow, that DOES help!" She took a couple more deep breaths. Then she began to tell us about how she hadn't just been mad about the game or about the rarewolf. She was nervous about meeting a new friend, Ari, because she thought Ari wouldn't like her.

"But I probably made you not like me even more," Lyssa moaned.

"That's not true! I like you, Lyssa. You're smart, and you stand up for yourself. I like that."

Lyssa blushed. "Thanks."

"Is that why you were upset when you got here, Lyssa? You were nervous about hanging out with Ari and me?"

"Sort of. But there was something else too. I was going to visit my old neighborhood this weekend and spend the night with my best friend from my old school. But then my momster told me I couldn't go after all because my grandma is coming to visit. I was really sad because I miss my friend a lot, so I yelled at my momster on the way over here."

"I'm sorry," I told her. "I would be really sad too."

"I'm really sorry I got mad at everybody."

We told her it was okay. Then came my idea.

"Hey, I want to show you something," Ari said. She pulled her fearometer out of her pocket. "I use this when I don't know what to do with my feelings. I match how scared or anxious I feel with one of the four colors. Once I know what color I'm feeling, I can decide what to do about it." She handed it to Lyssa for a closer look.

"Earlier, when I hurt your feelings and was afraid you hated me, I decided I felt Yellow. So that meant I needed to use ST_4 to stop and think about what I did and how I could make it better. I told myself that you probably didn't hate me over one silly game. At least, I hope that's true!"

"I don't hate you!" Lyssa exclaimed.

Ari beamed.

I chimed in. "One time we all had to give presentations in front of our monsterology class, and Ari was really nervous because she hates speaking in front of people. But she used her fearometer, and that helped her face her fear."

"Yep. I took a LOT of deep breaths that day," Ari said, pointing to Orange on her fearometer.

"She was CLAWESOME!" I jumped up and pumped my fists in the air. Ari giggled.

Lyssa looked much less upset now, her eyes wide with excitement. "Can you teach me how to make one, Ari?" she begged. "I really think a fearometer will help me. I'm nervous for the Scare Fair tomorrow and, as you saw, I'm not really in charge of my body and my feelings right now."

"Yes, of course I can teach you!"

So that's how we spent the rest of the afternoon—horns-deep in art supplies, making fearometers. Lyssa went home that night with a bounce in her step and a paper fearometer in her hand.

CHAPTER 15:

Another Shiny Idea

The big day was FINALLY here! The school gym (where the Scare Fair was being held) was alive with colorful displays, with horrible and delightful smells, and with all sorts of sciency sounds like fizzing and popping and squealing and buzzing.

Parents, teachers, and monsters roamed from table to table. It felt like the whole school was there!

I was nervous. That must have meant Lyssa was even MORE nervous. But to my surprise, she ran up to me with a big grin on her face, already talking a monster-mile a minute.

"I was thinking about everything we talked about yesterday, about the fearometer and taking deep breaths and time-ins. Then I remembered what you said about rockets and emotions, and I thought of a BRILLIANT idea!"

Whenever Lyssa was happy, things were always BRILLIANT! She was right, though—when she told me what her idea was, I thought it was BRILLIANT too!

The sights and sounds of the Scare Fair filled me up with extra energy. As if I needed any more of that! I watched the judges prowl from booth to booth, whispering to each other, scribbling furiously on clipboards.

Then I wandered off to watch Felix Furryman race different cars down a track to see which materials would go faster—a metal car? A wooden car?

I got so distracted that I lost track of time and almost didn't make it back for OUR presentation! I dashed back to our table, bracing myself for a blowup from Lyssa—but it didn't come. She was smiling confidently at the judges who were approaching.

It was finally our turn!

CHAPTER 16:

In Which Lyssa and I Sound Impressive

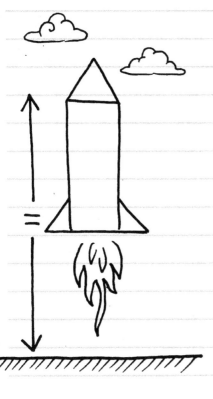

"Rockets rely on Spewton's Third Law of Motion to launch," Lyssa began. "Every action has an equal and opposite reaction. Rockets heat up gases that shoot out the bottom of the rocket.

"The force of the expelled gases pushes down on the ground, so the equal and opposite reaction is that the rocket is pushed high into the air." Our rocket stood on its stand—looking proud, as if it knew we were talking about it.

I then explained that space shuttles, once in space, need to go 17,000 monster-miles per hour to stay in Monstearth's orbit! I told the crowd everything I learned about how shuttles re-enter Monstearth's atmosphere and then land.

"This part is important, because if a space shuttle doesn't slow down enough, it will smash into the ground. SPLOOSH!!" I smacked my hands together and made a smashing noise. I giggled. "As space shuttles fall back to Monstearth, they use turns and tilts to slow down. Then a giant parachute pops out the back to slow things down even more so the shuttle can land safely."

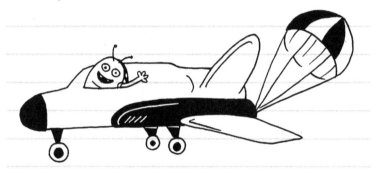

Lyssa spoke again. "All of this is helpful to know, even if you're not a monsternaut. For example, sometimes I get mad—really steaming, screaming mad. But learning about rockets and space shuttles helped me think of a new way to look at my angry feelings."

"Maybe my emotions are like a rocket. The more that they heat up and launch sky-high, the more it pushes the ground away—like Spewton's Third Law of Motion."

Wow, was Lyssa amazing! She sounded so smart. The judges were astonished at the sudden twist, whispering to each other.

"But what's on the ground while my emotions are sky-high? My family is. My friends." (She smiled at me for that part!) "School. Music. My other hobbies. Things that make me happy. So, the bigger my reaction—like when I get mad and blow up—the more I push away things that should be making me happy, like playing games with my friend Marvin," she said, pointing to me.

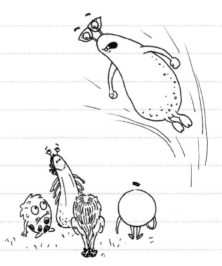

"And that's where the parachute comes in!" I blurted.

"Exactly," Lyssa said. "My friends Marvin and Harriet taught me ways I can recognize and handle my anger. And I came up with one of my own. These things are parachutes that carry me safely back down to Monstearth."

Do you think she's talking about ST4, the fearometer, or time-ins?

All of them!

Now I was ready to burst from excitement. "And now, monsters and monstresses, if you'll follow us outside," I announced.

The judges, Mrs. Grimm, and several curious classmates happily did. We set up our rocket on the large, empty blacktop.

"Time for the moment you've all been waiting for . . ." Lyssa announced dramatically. Mrs. Grimm stepped forward and lit the fuse on our rocket.

Suddenly my stomach did loop-de-loops and corkscrews like a terrorific looper coaster. I hadn't stopped to think about what would happen during the launch. We only had one chance to get it right! What if it exploded? What if it didn't work at all? What if it hit the school?

But wait—Mrs. Grimm knew all about
our project and knew adults would be there
in case something happened. And Lyssa
definitely knew what she was doing—I had
no doubt. I took a deep breath.

And in a huge puff of smoke, our rocket shot high into the sky, squealing and hissing! Everyone cheered—Lyssa and me the loudest! It may not have been the best-looking rocket ever made—definitely not as good as the first one I decorated—but it didn't matter now, because it was nearly out of sight! Maybe it would go all the way to outer space, never to be seen again!

But a moment later, the distant dot over our heads began to grow bigger. Soon we could see a slender shape floating steadily to the ground with the help of a parachute. Lyssa and I ran to catch it. It landed on the triple-tailed monkey bars on the playground!

We brought the rocket back to a clapping, cheering, whooping crowd—especially Mrs. Grimm! The judges looked truly impressed.

"Lyssa, Marvin, that was WONDERFUL!" Mrs. Grimm gushed. "What a fine idea to bring the psychological sciences into your science project!"

Lyssa and I looked at each other and grinned. We hadn't planned it that way before this morning, but in the end, we definitely learned about more than just rockets!

CHAPTER 17

A Real
Claw-Biter

The time had finally arrived! One last thing remained: the results.

Everyone gathered in the gymnasium as Mrs. Grimm made her way to the podium. I found my mind drifting to thoughts of glory. We had already impressed an adoring crowd—now to get our gold medals and the grand prize!

Mrs. Grimm thanked all the participants and teachers for some "truly impressive displays." She continued, "It was a difficult decision to choose a first-place winner. The judges debated and discussed many projects that were well developed and terrorific. Many entries were creative, challenging, and thought provoking. But there was one outstanding project that the judges have chosen to award first place.

"And the winners are . . ." (I could scarcely breathe!)

"Tyler Terror and Nella Nasty, for a truly disgusting display on fungus and mold!"

The audience cheered and hollered. Confetti fell from the ceiling all around me. I felt my heart drop like a boulder to my stomach. I turned to Lyssa. Her mouth was wide open with disbelief.

"I . . . I thought everyone loved ours," I stammered.

There was no mistake. Tyler and Nella were grinning and waving happily from the stage. They had won the grand prize—gold medals, a day off school, a field trip of their choice, and fame and glory for the rest of their time in middle school and maybe their lives.

I turned to Lyssa again only to see her weaving through the crowd away from me. Her skin color changed to blue, then gray, then black, then blue again.

I followed her and found her sitting on a bench with her head in her hands. I hesitated before sitting down beside her. What if she lashed out and hit me or something?

She didn't. We just sat while the audience went wild, followed by Mrs. Grimm giving a speech I barely heard.

"Rat guts," I said. "I really thought we had that one."

Lyssa looked up. Her eyes were wet, but she wasn't crying. "Me too."

We sat quietly for a few minutes while the crowd chattered happily. Perhaps Lyssa was doing a time-in.

"Are you okay?" Lyssa finally asked. I was surprised—I usually asked HER that, not the other way around.

"Yeah, I think so. Just disappointed."

Someone tapped me on the shoulder. It was Felix from my garbageball team, and Heidi was with him.

"We thought you two would win," Felix said.
"I can't believe you two made a rocket
that could actually fly!"

"Yeah!" Heidi agreed. "And I've never
thought about feelings being like a rocket.
That was frightfully cool."

"Thanks," Lyssa and I said. I wasn't sure
if I felt better or worse.

"Wait!" Mrs. Grimm called suddenly
into the microphone. "We have one more
announcement to make!"

CHAPTER 18

Monstrous Character

When the gasps and curious chatter finally quieted, Mrs. Grimm began. "Monsters and monstresses, for the first time ever, the judges have decided to give an additional award."

An additional award? Mrs. Grimm had never said anything about that!

"In addition to recognizing the top-scoring science project, we have decided to recognize two very special individuals who have learned about more than just science. They discovered that you cannot always avoid failure, even when you're trying your best. They learned about perseverance. They learned how to be kind, how to forgive, and how to cope with difficult circumstances, even when an unfortunate accident destroyed the first version of a truly impressive rocket. Lyssa, Marvin, would you come forward, please?"

Wait, WHAT?! My stomach knotted. Lyssa, suddenly pink in the face, looked as stunned as I did! Astonished, we crept up to the stage while people all around clapped and cheered.

"I have been carefully watching their progress. Creating a second rocket was difficult, and they had very little time to do it. But they succeeded! In fact, I believe their second project turned out all the better because of what they discovered along the way. They went the extra mile by sharing what they learned about managing their emotions. They are a shining example of teamwork, creativity, and compassion. For that, we have decided to award them the Monstrous Character Award."

The crowd clapped and whistled! Lyssa and I just stared at each other in shock.

Mrs. Grimm handed each of us a dino egg.
They were black with colorful swirls and
tiny yellow specks all over them.

"It looks like a galaxy!" Lyssa marveled.

"Exactly," Mrs. Grimm said. "We wanted
you to have something to help you remember

your project and what you learned: that the most important thing in life is having good character."

Now I was embarrassed! Mrs. Grimm had never said so many nice things to me all at once!

"In addition, the school will send you two with a parent to the planetarium, where you can learn about intergalactic monstro-cities and see spooktacular meteor light shows. You may go any weekend you desire," Mrs. Grimm explained.

"Aww, not during school?!" I blurted out.

Everyone laughed—even Mrs. Grimm!
"Sorry, not this time, Marvin." She
smiled warmly. "Everyone, please join me in
congratulating Marvin and Lyssa."

Everyone clapped, snorted, whistled, and
whooped. I felt my spirits soar above the
clouds, like our rocket did!

Ari found us as we made our way through
the crowd. "You two were SO clawesome!
Your rocket was positively FRIGHTFUL!"
Ari exclaimed. Timmy joined in, clapping me
on the back and saying, "I knew you guys
would do horrorifically!"

Our parents, beaming with pride, found us and gave us each big monster-bear hugs.

"I'm so proud of you, sweetheart," Lyssa's mom said as she hugged her daughter. "Your project was stunning. And I saw how you kept your cool when your project didn't win first place." She gave her daughter an extra squeeze.

"You make your scientist father proud, son," Popster said with a big pat on my back.

Lyssa and I were smiling like we'd never smiled before. Then we wound up and gave each other the most epic high four EVER!

Even though our rocket didn't technically win, it sure was clawfuls of fun. (Mostly.) I'd never been to a planetarium before, but I knew it was going to be monsterific. After all, my new friend Lyssa would be right there with me!

Make Your Own ST₄ Badges

Ask an adult to help you photocopy these ST₄ badges. Color them however you'd like, cut them out, and then tape or pin them wherever you need a reminder!

Resources for Parents and Teachers

Welcome to our community of parents striving to raise happy, bubbly, successful, mindful children with all kinds of minds. Children need to recognize their innate power, learn to be in charge of their own bodies, and learn how to turn challenging situations around. Yet being able to live in the now and appreciate the wonder of the moment while at the same time being aware of one's emotional state can be a challenge for many of us.

To guide children gently—not by pulling or shoving but rather with a gentle nudge of the elbow and a reassuring word—along their own path to the self-realization that they are beautiful and gifted, regardless of faults or foibles, should be the goal of every mindful parent. So how is that done? Let your child know, with specific praise for specific actions, that they are accepted unconditionally while at the same time teaching them the tools necessary to navigate the challenges of life.

We all need to know what is expected of us, how to read our own signals and impulses, when to put on the brakes, when to slow down, and when to let off steam. We basically need to learn how to be mindful. This goal is not easily or quickly achieved, but that is the purpose of this book and the ST_4 Mindfulness Books for Kids series.

What about ADHD?

Children with ADHD are inattentive, distractible, restless, and have difficulty sitting still. They appear to be in constant motion. They may interrupt, blurt out comments, have trouble focusing, and struggle waiting their turn. In addition, they are often easily stressed and quick to anger. ADHD rarely travels alone. We call the associated challenges co-occurring disorders. Anger and anxiety are two common examples of these. These symptoms can be present without ADHD being diagnosed, but in this section of the book, we will focus on those children who have both sets of symptoms.

Families sometimes struggle when a child has ADHD. Brothers and sisters will often complain that their sibling always spoils everything or always wants to fight. In many cases, children with ADHD crave the rush of the fight to keep them awake and alert. Picking fights is just one way they might do this—exasperating everyone in the family, their friends, and their teachers. Angry outbursts almost appear to be the rule rather than the exception in children with ADHD.

What Is Anger, and What Triggers Angry Outbursts?

Who of us has not had an angry outburst? Call it a "wobbly," a meltdown, a temper tantrum, a hissie fit. Why do we do that? And why do children in particular have these intense emotional outbursts?

Are some children more susceptible to being angry? Temperament differences are evident very early on. Some infants appear easygoing, others are slow to warm up, and others exhibit characteristics that would translate as "being difficult." Those children might later have emotional ups and downs with little capacity to respond appropriately to stressful situations. These characteristics could be considered innate, but environmental factors can also impact an individual's capacity to regulate emotional responses. There might be other reasons for anger, including family dysfunction and genetic predispositions.

Stress is what happens when demands are placed upon us to adapt to the world and to various situations. A common response to stress in both adults and children is anger. That anger can come across as being oppositional or defiant. Thus, when a parent informs me of oppositional and defiant behaviors in their child, we begin to consider what might be stressing that child.

It's important to distinguish between anger and aggression. Anger is a temporary emotional state caused by stress, worry, or frustration. It's a way our minds warn us of potential problems. We all get angry. It's an emotion seen in all children and adults—in fact, it's a normal and even healthy feeling. Most children either respond appropriately to angry feelings or can learn to do so.

Aggression, however, is usually an active attempt to hurt or destroy things, often as a response to anger. When the intensity of any behavior is concerning or potentially harmful, seek help from your doctor.

Parenting a Child Who Is Susceptible to Angry Outbursts

We know that talking about feelings helps calm the waters. Reassurance goes a long way; it is one of the cornerstones of nurturing parenting. Let children know that having angry feelings is normal and that everyone experiences them. Reassure them that you will do your best to make the world a safer place for them and that you are there to help and comfort them. Tell them about the times you yourself have had angry feelings and about your own coping strategies that you use in those situations—like reciting a mantra or practicing breathing when feeling angry or stressed. It's surprising how many adults continue to use the words they learned from their loving parents in early childhood.

Let your child know that sometimes we feel bad, grumpy, tearful, or upset—and we don't always know why.

Good news: we can learn to recognize signals of anger and stress, and then we can learn to do something about them. We will need the right tools to tackle this problem. Just letting your child know you understand them and teaching them about recognizing feelings can be so helpful. Knowledge is a powerful coping tool.

Signs a Child May Have Anger Issues

- Has frequent angry outbursts, even over minor issues
- Is unable to explain feelings when upset
- Has trouble calming down when frustrated
- Exhibits physical aggression such as hitting, fighting, kicking, shouting, swearing, tantrums
- Doesn't seem to care about people's feelings
- Doesn't accept responsibility for aggression; blames others
- Has trouble bouncing back from frustrations
- Acts without thinking
- Acts super sullen and silent and holds in feelings
- Talks, writes, or draws pictures about violence
- Bullies or acts aggressively toward others

Assume that all behaviors have some underlying communicative intent. That will help make sense of behavior and make it easier to understand, empathize with, and manage. By viewing the behavior from the outside and not getting embroiled in one's own angry feelings, we will be in a much better position to view the behavior objectively and be more effective in managing the behavior. The first step is to determine why the behavior might be happening. Angry outbursts can be a response to danger or simply a person's way of asserting themselves. In childhood particularly, anger could be a statement of independence.

There are multiple triggers to anger:

- Anxiety (in my experience, this is the most common trigger)
- Bullying and teasing at school
- Doing undesired tasks
- Having to accept "no" for an answer
- Perception of danger
- Sensory overload
- Not being able to choose the agenda
- Attention seeking
- Special challenges
- Low self-esteem
- Sadness or depression (what adults may experience as sadness is often expressed by a child as anger)
- Added stresses within the home (e.g., parent conflict, a new baby)

Using the Feelings Toolbox

There are two key steps in anger and stress management. The first is to help the child identify the feelings they are having using "I feel . . ." statements—the "I feel . . ." step. The second step is the "I can . . ." step, where the child learns and uses coping strategies to manage those feelings.

Step 1: "I Feel . . ."

First, help your child identify their feelings. Give voice to their emotions. "I can see that you are angry right now." Try to identify the triggers that set off these feelings; statements like "you are angry because . . ." are helpful. "You are mad because your brother hit you" or "you feel that things are unfair" are also examples.

Parents can teach this first basic step of managing angry feelings or stress regardless of age or ability.

Whether speaking aloud or saying the words in our mind, sometimes simply saying "I feel . . . " can be enough to cut through the confusion and settle our worries, or at least reduce them.

Everyone (children and adults) experiences angry feelings or stress differently. Some kids make their muscles tight like a suit of armor (like what happens if someone is going to hit you in the stomach). Some breathe fast or hold their breath. Some get red in the face and have a headache.

Describing how you feel is an excellent way of getting in touch with your emotional state. For many children, angry feelings can be overwhelming and mystifying. But once children can label these symptoms, they are in touch with their feelings. It moves angry thoughts and feelings from their gut and into their heads, and they can now be mindful. So, if a child feels angry with a thumping heart and a red face it doesn't mean everyone will hate them or that a disaster will strike or that the sky will fall in. It just means that they are upset or stressed. Then they can say "I feel upset!" or "I feel angry." Recognizing and labelling those feelings is exactly what we want them to do—to express their anger instead of lashing out or holding the anger in. Statements such as "I don't like it when you take my stuff," or "I don't feel like sharing right now" can help.

Have your child answer the questions below when they feel upset, angry or stressed:

DOES YOUR BODY EVER FEEL LIKE ANY OF THESE?
- Head full of aches
- Tummy full of butterflies
- Heart full of thumps

- Hands full of sweat
- Face full of red
- Muscles full of tightness
- Nights full of scares

DO YOU OFTEN FEEL . . .
- mad and angry?
- afraid and worried?
- sad and tearful?
- frustrated and irritable?
- quiet and shy?

DO YOU OFTEN . . .
- feel scared of talking in front of the class?
- forget things?
- feel picked on?
- take jokes too seriously?
- worry whether people like you?

If your child experiences several of these feelings and symptoms, it may mean that they are stressed. Have them say it out loud: "I am angry," or "I am stressed."

Step 2: "I Can . . ."

Next, help your child determine how to cope. That's when we say, "I can . . ." We will discuss tools that children can use to cope with stress and fears.

Again, let your child know that you yourself often have similar feelings of anger. Practice talking out loud when stressful events happen to you, such as getting cut off while driving in the car. Demonstrate how you can state the problem, identify the feeling, and come up with a solution.

Many parents were not taught how to deal with anger during childhood. Being angry was akin to being bad and was a source of guilty feelings. Let us allow children to feel all their feelings. Adults can show children acceptable ways of expressing their feelings. Strong feelings cannot be denied, and angry outbursts should be recognized and treated with respect.

Here's where you help your child learn what to do about their feelings. This is where we figure out the tools that will best work for your child.

Breath awareness, body awareness, and mind awareness are three tools that help children manage angry feelings or stress. Here's how:

BREATH AWARENESS

Take a slow, deep breath. Count to 4 as you breathe in all the way, and then count to 4 as you slowly breathe out. Feel your body relax. Say, "I am the boss of my body." Do this 5 times. Even doing it one time helps your body relax.

BODY AWARENESS

Tighten the muscles in your face, squeeze your eyes shut, and bite your teeth tight. Hold this for 3 seconds. Relax those muscles and feel the difference in your face. Do this 3 times. Now tighten your fists, arms, and stomach. Hold for 3 seconds and relax. Do this 3 times. Squeeze your legs together and point your toes. Hold for 3 seconds and relax. Repeat the exercise 3 times. How does that feel?

MIND AWARENESS

After you control your breath and muscles, it is time to relax your mind. Think of a nice, calm place—maybe a beach or a forest, or even your room! Imagine you are there now. Imagine what that place looks like. Try to hear what that place sounds like. Tell yourself, "I can control my body and my mind. I can calm myself down when I get upset." Say this over and over to yourself, or recite another phrase, mantra, or prayer that comforts you or helps you feel more confident.

Schedule a time to practice these tools at least once a day. Bedtime works well. Continue practicing them throughout the day as well, like at school or in the car. Using these tools will soon help you handle daily stress. You will find that some tools work better than others. Pay attention to this. What works when? Which tools do you like best?

The Feelings Fearometer

The **Feelings Fearometer** is used to combine the "I feel" and "I can" tools. It helps children grade or color-code the intensity of their feelings and decide which coping tools to use to address those feelings.

1) Draw a thermometer in the shape of a test-tube or an old-fashioned thermometer and divide it into four sections.

2) For the first or bottom section, choose a color that reminds you of feeling calm (e.g., green). Label this section 1.

3) Now choose the color you feel when you are beginning to feel nervous (e.g., yellow). Label this section 2.

4) The third section will be the color you feel when you are really stressed (e.g., orange). Label this section 3.

5) The top level will be the color they feel when they are most stressed (e.g., fire-engine red!). Label this section 4.

6) To the left of the fearometer, create a column labeled "I feel." Next to each section, write down the feelings or physical symptoms your child typically experiences for that level.

7) To the right of the fearometer, create a column labeled "I can." Next to each section, come up with coping skills appropriate to that color or level of stress. They could

range from Breath Awareness for level 2 all the way to taking a shower for level 4!

Note: Creating the complete fearometer is not always easy, but the project does not have to be completed in one sitting!

Routine and rhythms are often lost at times of stress and anger—even our biorhythms. We breathe faster, our pulse races, not to mention that sleep and bowel rhythms are altered. As your child learns the tools of breath, body, and mind awareness, make sure your child maintains routine, a healthy diet, and plenty of rest. Activities that enhance rhythmicity are very calming; activities such as playing music, swinging, biking, and rhythmical sports like swimming should all be encouraged.

What Else Can Your Child Do?

Lyssa learns another strategy in this book—ST_4! This was introduced by Marvin and Timmy in earlier books. It is designed to enhance mindfulness and self-awareness. Giving a child tools for changing situations that are uncomfortable for them engages them in the treatment process and assures them that we are on their side and that we do understand the challenges they are having.

ST_4

How to use ST_4:

- Let your child know that they can learn to control their body and what comes out of their mouth. Even control their thoughts! That is empowering.
- Explain what a "formula" is, like how water is H_2O and oxygen is O_2. If that concept is too abstract, just stick to the numbers and letters.

- Explain what ST_4 stands for. STOP what they are doing—that's the S. Then they need to TAKE TIME TO THINK. Count the T's—that's four, right? One S and four T's—that's why we say ST_4.
- Emblazon that formula on stickers or badges.
- Place the stickers on backpacks, folders, school desks, or the bathroom mirror!

It can be helpful to tell teachers about ST_4; they might use it in the classroom. The teacher can simply point to the sticker on the child's desk as needed.

The formula can be kept a secret if your child prefers. Keeping it secret allows the child to develop a positive rapport with the teacher while avoiding any unnecessary humiliation by being called out publicly.

Calming Strategies

What about in the classroom? Speak to your child's teacher about allowing a "time-*in*." Maybe allow the child to leave the room, lie down, or walk outside. Separate those who are acting aggressively. Some teachers establish chill spaces where children can go to cool down and gain control. Call it the calm spot. Provide a bean bag, books, music, headphones, and crayons.

At home, parents can help the child find the most effective way to calm anger. The child could draw a picture of their feelings, pound clay, hit a pillow, shoot baskets, punch a punching bag, or even talk to themselves.

Teach children to try to understand why others might not be doing what they would like them to do. Think of solutions, like the child apologizing for getting angry. Ask your child to draw or write what is upsetting them on a piece of paper. Then have them tear it into little pieces and "throw the anger away."

Teach a simple message or mantra your child can say in stressful situations. For example: "Stop and calm down," "Stay in control," or "I can handle this." Maybe even ST_4!

Relaxation Strategies

Here is a relaxation exercise that you can read to your child:

Let's spend a few minutes together, focusing on how you can relax your body and gain control over your thinking. Try this activity whenever you start to feel irritable, angry, tense, or worried.

Get as comfortable as you can. Good. Close your eyes and take some slow and deep breaths. Take a deep breath in, and then pretend to blow out a long string of bubbles into the air. Take another deep breath in, and slowly blow out another string of bubbles. Imagine the bubbles floating off into the air. See how shiny and colorful the bubbles look.

Slowly take another deep breath in, and slowly continue to blow out bubbles. Feel how your body is nice and calm. Feel your muscles soften, and notice how you feel more and more comfortable. You are now relaxed.

Practice taking deep breaths and slowly breathing out bubbles at any time. You are in charge of your body and how you feel.

What Else Can Parents Do?

Dear Parent: First take a deep breath before you intervene. Remember you are the adult and the kind teacher here. Rise to the occasion. Breathe again.

Remember that you want to reach, teach, and protect your children—not punish them.

Tell them what other children do when they feel like this. Read a book (like this one!) about what some children do when they feel angry. Teach acceptable ways of coping. Discover ways to communicate what is expected.

Things to Remember When Your Child Is Dealing with Anger

- **Set limits.** Let children know who's in charge—"If you won't stop it, I will."
- **Follow through with consequences.** Say "NO!" and mean it!
- **Be firm and clear.**
- **Forgive.** Forgiving your child helps them move from guilt to hope.
- **Have faith.** Bad behavior is not the same as a bad person.
- **Catch the child being good.** Identify eight positive behaviors before identifying a negative one. A great ratio!
- **Don't sweat the small stuff.** Ignore behavior that can be tolerated.
- **Anticipate challenging times.**
- **Use closeness and touching—show affection.** Sometimes a hug is all that is needed.
- **Give the child a way out.** Let them save face.
- **Use promises and rewards.** Use these to start and to stop behavior. Always deliver on your promises.
- **Use punishment cautiously.** Remember to discipline means to teach. Punishment is not a helpful strategy to teach coping skills. Never use physical punishment.

Children such as Lyssa need to know they are not alone in their struggles. They need to know they are just as smart as other kids, just as funny and creative, just as loveable, and just as likely to succeed. A focus on the positive will help bolster self-esteem and confidence in children dealing with anger—these children often suffer enormously from being constantly berated and being in trouble.

Labels aren't necessary, but self-awareness and awareness of challenges are. If we can name it, we can tame it. That is the lesson for Lyssa and Marvin in this book. Teach kids about the power within them to take charge of their own bodies! That is precisely the point of ST_4 and the tools that are taught in this book.

Of course, this will not take place overnight, but teaching your children coping tools early and then frequently reinforcing them will go a long way. If we can do that without being patronizing, and all the while helping improve self-esteem, then we surely must be on the right path. The tools taught here will foster in children a sense of competency, an ability to identify their strengths, and the development of appropriate coping strategies.

The way to take control is to get the best treatment for ADHD, whether that be medication, counseling, cognitive behavioral therapy, or coaching. Wouldn't it indeed also be wonderful to allow children a modicum of control over their own selves? To become mindful? That's where this book comes in!

About the Authors and Illustrator

Dr. Raun Melmed

Raun D. Melmed, MD, FAAP, a developmental and behavioral pediatrician, is director of the Melmed Center in Scottsdale, Arizona, and cofounder and medical director of the Southwest Autism Research and Resource Center. He is the author of *Autism: Early Intervention*; *Autism and the Extended Family*; and a series of books on mindfulness for children: *Marvin's Monster Diary: ADHD Attacks, Timmy's Monster Diary: Screen Time Stress, Harriet's Monster Diary: Awfully Anxious*, and the next in the series, *Marvin's Monster Diary 2 (+Lyssa): ADHD Emotion Explosion*.

Caroline Bliss Larsen

Caroline Bliss Larsen edits BYU Independent Study courses by day and writes and edits novels by night. She is also a freelance acquiring editor for Jolly Fish Press and Flux, imprints of North Star Editions. She holds a BA in English language from Brigham Young University, with minors in editing and English literature. *Marvin's Monster Diary 2 (+ Lyssa)* is her debut novel. Follow her on Twitter @editor_caro or visit carolineblisslarsen.com.

Arief Kriembonga

Arief Kriembonga graduated from Jakarta Arts Institute, Indonesia. He started his career as a children's and comic book illustrator in 2010. In addition to being an illustrator, Arief also works as a UI/UX and graphic designer. Besides art, his greatest passion is single-origin coffee. He lives with his wife and one beloved daughter in Jakarta, Indonesia.

About Familius

Familius is a global-trade publishing company that publishes books and other content to help families be happy. We believe that the family is the fundamental unit of society and that happy families are the foundation of a happy life. We recognize that every family looks different, and we passionately believe in helping all families find greater joy. To that end, we publish books for children and adults that invite families to live the Familius Nine Habits of Happy Family Life: *love together, play together, learn together, work together, talk together, heal together, read together, eat together,* and *laugh together.* Founded in 2012, Familius is located in Sanger, California.

Connect

WEBSITE: WWW.FAMILIUS.COM

FACEBOOK: WWW.FACEBOOK.COM/PATERFAMILIUS

TWITTER: @FAMILIUSTALK, @PATERFAMILIUS1

PINTEREST: WWW.PINTEREST.COM/FAMILIUS

FAMILIUS

**The most important work you
ever do will be within the walls
of your own home.**

CPSIA information can be obtained
at www.ICGtesting.com
Printed in the USA
FSHW020029280619

9 781641 701365